NANCY DREW

girl detective®

P9-DOE-115

CHASE BRANCH LIBRARY
17731 W. SEVEN MILE RD.
DETROIT, MI 48235

FEB 2007

0453288 05

NANCY DREW

girl detective®

Graphic Novels
Available from Papercutz

#1 The Demon of River Heights
#2 Writ In Stone
#3 The Haunted Dollhouse
#4 The Girl Who Wasn't There
(coming February 2006)

$7.95 each in paperback
$12.95 each in hardcover

Please add $3.00 for postage and handling for the first book, add $1.00 for each additional book.

Send for our catalog:
Papercutz
555 Eighth Avenue, Suite 1202
New York, NY 10018
www.papercutz.com

NANCY DREW

#3 girl detective®

The Old Fashioned Mystery of the Haunted Dollhouse

STEFAN PETRUCHA • Writer
SHO MURASE • Artist
with 3D CG elements by RACHEL ITO
Based on the series by
CAROLYN KEENE

New York

The Haunted Dollhouse
STEFAN PETRUCHA – Writer
SHO MURASE – Artist
with 3D CG elements by RACHEL ITO
BRYAN SENKA – Letterer
CARLOS JOSE GUZMAN
SHO MURASE
Colorists
JIM SALICRUP
Editor-in-Chief

ISBN 10: 1-59707-008-4 paperback edition
ISBN 13: 978-1-59707-008-9 paperback edition
ISBN 10: 1-59707-009-2 hardcover edition
ISBN 13: 978-1-59707-009-6 hardcover edition

Copyright © 2005 by Simon & Schuster, Inc. Published by arrangement with Aladdin Paperbacks, an imprint of Simon & Schuster Children's Publishing Division.
Nancy Drew is a trademark of Simon & Schuster, Inc.
All rights reserved.

Printed in China.

10 9 8 7 6 5 4 3 2 1

NANCY DREW HERE. IT DOESN'T TAKE A DETECTIVE TO FIGURE OUT THAT YOU'RE PROBABLY WONDERING WHY I'M DRIVING THIS VINTAGE ***ROADSTER*** INSTEAD OF MY TRUSTY HYBRID.

WELL, MR. DAVE CRABTREE, AN ANTIQUE CAR DEALER, AND A CLIENT OF MY FATHER'S, ***LOANED*** IT TO ME. IN FACT, A FEW HOURS AGO HE LOANED OUT ***ALL*** HIS CARS.

NOPE, HE HASN'T GONE NUTS! IT'S ALL PART OF RIVER HEIGHTS ***NOSTALGIA*** WEEK!

EVERYONE PARTICIPATING (AND THAT'S MOST OF THE CITY!) IS WEARING 1930s CLOTHES AND USING PERIOD TECHNOLOGY TO CELEBRATE THE CREATION OF THE ***STRATEMEYER FOUNDATION*** IN 1930.

CHAPTER ONE:
WHAT A DOLLHOUSE!

OUR HOUSEKEEPER, HANNAH, FOUND THE DREW FAMILY CONTRIBUTION, THIS OLD CLOCK UP IN THE ATTIC.
THE WEEK ENDS WITH AN ANTIQUE AUCTION - ALL THE PROCEEDS GOING TO THE FOUNDATION.
I WAS ON MY WAY TO DROP IT OFF AT CITY HALL AND WATCH THE OPENING CEREMONIES, LITTLE REALIZING A VINTAGE MYSTERY WAS ABOUT TO TAKE PLACE!
EVEN MY BEST PALS GEORGE AND BESS GOT INTO THE ACT.
ANTIQUES
SO, WHAT'S BUZZIN' COUSINS?
YIKES! CHECK OUT THOSE SPIFFY WHEELS!
HMM... BETTER GO EASY ON THE GAS, OR YOU COULD BLOW A BABBIT!
SOME PEOPLE WOULDN'T THINK A REAL DOLL, AS THEY USED TO SAY, LIKE BESS WOULD HAVE SUCH A KNACK WITH MACHINES, BUT SHE DOES!
OH, AND A BABBIT IS A SPECIAL ALLOY USED IN OLD CAR BEARINGS TO REDUCE THE FRICTION OF MOVING PARTS.

GREAT. NANCY GETS A TERRIFIC CAR, BUT I CAN'T EVEN USE MY CELL!
I CAN'T BELIEVE I LET YOU GUYS TALK ME INTO GIVING UP MY COMPUTER FOR A WHOLE WEEK! I MEAN, THAT'S LIKE ASKING NANCY TO GIVE UP MYSTERIES!
OH, YOU'RE JUST BEING A PARTY-POOPER!
I LOVE THIS OLD STUFF! THE 78 RPM RECORDS, THE OLD PHONES!
CAN YOU BELIEVE THEY USED TO MAKE RECORDINGS ON WIRES?
OKAY GALS, THIS THING IS HEAVY, SO WHAT SAY WE SHAKE A LEG AND GET OVER TO TOWN HALL?
RIVERSIDE
SHAKE A WHAT?
1930s SLANG - IT MEANS LET'S GET GOING! SO LET'S!

THE FRONT OF CITY HALL HAD ALSO BEEN MADE TO MATCH THE MOOD. EVEN THE STREET LAMPS HAD BEEN REPLACED.
TOWN
SO LET ME NOT WASTE ANY TIME IN INTRODUCING MY PARTNER IN THIS AFFAIR, ***MRS. EMMA BLAVATSKY***!
MRS. CORNELIUS MAHONEY, WHO RUNS JUST ABOUT EVERY CHARITY EVENT IN RH, WAS BEHIND THIS ONE, TOO – BUT THIS TIME SHE HAD HELP FROM A ***NEWCOMER***.

THANK YOU, AGNES. AS YOU KNOW, THE COLLINS ESTATE I RECENTLY PURCHASED WAS BUILT IN 1933.
SO I THOUGHT IT WOULD BE APPROPRIATE TO PUT THIS ***WONDERFUL*** ARCHITECT'S ***MODEL*** ON DISPLAY HERE.
I DIDN'T KNOW MRS. BLAVATSKY. SHE SEEMED SWEET, IF A LITTLE ***SENILE***. I'D HEARD SHE WAS ***VERY*** SUPERSTITIOUS, AND BELIEVED ***SPIRITS*** SPOKE TO HER.

ACCORDING TO THE ***SPIRITS*** OF THE COLLINS CHILDREN I'VE SPOKEN TO THROUGH MY OUIJA BOARD, THEY ***PLAYED*** WITH IT AS A ***DOLLHOUSE***.
AS A MATTER OF FACT, I BELIEVE THE MODEL ***ITSELF*** MAY BE ***HAUNTED*** AND CAPABLE OF ***PREDICTING*** THE FUTURE!

HAUNTED?! GIVE ME A BREAK! THE OLD DAME IS DYING FOR ATTENTION.
WELL... BUT... HOW DO YOU REALLY KNOW?
I THINK THIS CALLS FOR A CLOSER LOOK!

CHECK OUT THE DETAILS! IT'S EVEN GOT A LITTLE HIDDEN STAIRCASE!
WAIT A MINUTE.

WHY IS THAT DOLL WEARING A MASK, LIKE A BURGLAR? IT LOOKS AS THOUGH IT'S STEALING THE PAINTING. AND THAT WINDOW'S BROKEN!
SHEESH! I SWEAR YOU SEE A MYSTERY IN EVERYTHING, NANCE! IT'S BEEN A FEW DAYS SINCE YOUR LAST CASE, SO YOU'RE JUST GETTING ANTSY!

GEORGE WASN'T KIDDING, I *DID* HAVE A NOSE FOR MYSTERIES. BUT SHE, OF ALL PEOPLE, SHOULD KNOW MY HUNCHES USUALLY PAY OFF.
CRASH
AND THIS TIME, AGAIN, IT TURNED OUT, I WAS *RIGHT*.

ACCORDING TO THE POLICE REPORT, AT ABOUT THE SAME TIME WE WERE SPEAKING, THE SILENCE AT THE *REAL* BLAVATSKY HOME WAS *SHATTERED* BY THE SOUND OF BREAKING GLASS!
AND THE CRIME HAPPENED *EXACTLY* THE SAME WAY IT DID IN THE DOLLHOUSE!

CREEPY, HUH?
SO, DID THIS MEAN THE MODEL REALLY WAS *HAUNTED*?

I, FOR ONE, DON'T *BELIEVE* IN GHOSTS! IN MY EXPERIENCE, THERE'S ALWAYS A SIMPLE, *REALISTIC* EXPLANATION - EVEN WHEN IT LOOKS LIKE THERE ISN'T.
BUT IT CERTAINLY WAS A *MYSTERY*, WHICH MEANT NEXT MORNING, I HEADED STRAIGHT FOR THE CRIME SCENE!
I WAS A LITTLE SURPRISED TO SEE THAT EVEN THE RIVER HEIGHTS POLICE WERE USING OLD STYLE CARS!

THANKS TO THE CRACKED WINDOW WHERE THE BURGLAR ENTERED, I COULD CLEARLY HEAR CHIEF McGINNIS TALKING TO EMMA BLAVATSKY INSIDE.
SOMETIMES THE CHIEF FILLS ME IN ON DETAILS, SOMETIMES HE *DOESN'T*, SO I DECIDED TO *EAVESDROP*.
THAT'S THE PROOF IT WAS GHOSTS! THE PAINTING WAS *WORTH-LESS*!

MY BROTHER PAINTED IT AS A CHILD. FOR YEARS WE KEPT IT IN THE FAMILY *BUNGALOW*. IT WAS JUST LAST WEEK I TOOK IT OUT OF STORAGE!
FOR SOME REASON, THE SPIRITS *ALWAYS* WANTED IT!

I KNOW I SHOULDN'T LAUGH AT OTHER PEOPLE'S BELIEFS, BUT POOR MRS. BLAVATSKY JUST SOUNDED KIND OF SILLY!

THAT IS, UNTIL SHE REALLY STARTED TALKING...
I KNOW YOU THINK ME SENILE, CHIEF, BUT IS IT SO HARD TO BELIEVE SOME PART OF US SURVIVES DEATH? NEARLY ALL RELIGIONS DO!
EVERYONE HAS AT LEAST ONE STORY WHERE THEY'VE SEEN SOME-THING THEY CAN'T EXPLAIN, OR FELT THE PRESENCE OF A DEAR DEPARTED STANDING NEAR.
THE AIR IS FULL OF THE ENERGIES OF THOSE WHO WALKED THE EARTH BEFORE US. I SPEAK TO THEM, SOMETIMES SEE THEM, AND I KNOW THEY ARE IN THAT DOLLHOUSE.

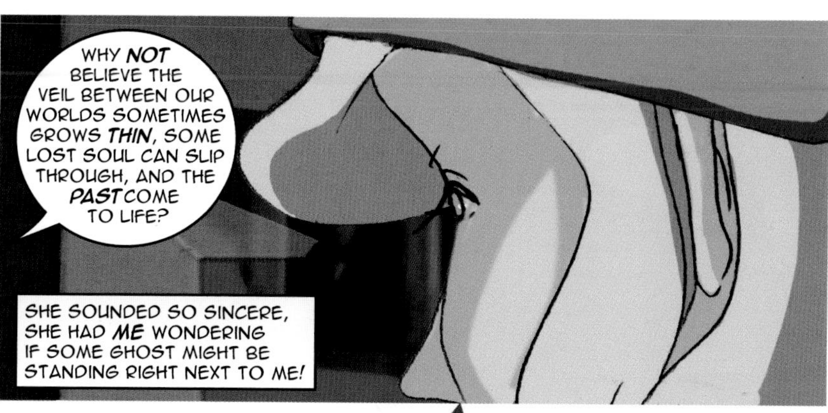
WHY NOT BELIEVE THE VEIL BETWEEN OUR WORLDS SOMETIMES GROWS THIN, SOME LOST SOUL CAN SLIP THROUGH, AND THE PAST COME TO LIFE?
SHE SOUNDED SO SINCERE, SHE HAD ME WONDERING IF SOME GHOST MIGHT BE STANDING RIGHT NEXT TO ME!

BOO!
AHHHH!

HA-HA-HA-HA!
SORRY, NANCY, I SAW YOU OUT HERE A WHILE AGO AND, SINCE I ALREADY FEEL LIKE I'M DRESSED FOR HALLOWEEN, I COULDN'T RESIST GIVING YOU A LITTLE SCARE!

SINCE YOU'RE HERE, WHY DON'T YOU COME INSIDE? MRS. BLAVATSKY HAS ALREADY ASKED FOR YOU!
I WAS THINKING ABOUT MENTIONING HOW STRANGE HE LOOKED IN HIS OLD HAT, BUT DECIDED THAT I SHOULDN'T - ESPECIALLY SINCE HE WAS LETTING ME INTO THE CRIME SCENE!

HI, MRS. BLAVATSKY.
NANCY DREW! SO MANY PEOPLE RESPECT YOU IN RIVER HEIGHTS, PERHAPS YOU CAN CONVINCE THEM THAT THE SPIRITS ARE BEHIND THIS THEFT!

WELL, I'M AFRAID, **FIRST** I'D HAVE TO CONVINCE **MYSELF**!
AND I'D NEED TO KNOW WHY, FOR INSTANCE, A **GHOST** WOULD HAVE TO BREAK A WINDOW!

OR LEAVE **FOOT-PRINTS**!
POOR DEAR! SOME-TIMES YOU JUST HAVE TO STOP **REASONING** TO SEE THE TRUTH!

THE SPIRITS CONTROLLED WHOEVER BROKE IN HERE! THEY TOLD ME SO THEMSELVES!
IF THEY GAVE YOU HIS NAME, WE COULD FIND HIM AND RETURN THE PAINTING!
ALAS, THEY DO NOT SPEAK THAT CLEARLY, EVEN TO ME!
I SUGGEST YOU RETURN TO THE DOLLHOUSE! IT MAY HOLD THE ANSWERS FOR YOU!
HA! HOW ABOUT ALL THAT SPIRIT TALK! IT WAS PROBABLY JUST SOME PETTY THIEF WHO STOLE THE WRONG PAINTING!
IF YOU ASK ME, EMMA BLAVATSKY'S A SWEET OLD LOON!
I WOULDN'T INSULT OTHER PEOPLE'S TASTE IF I WERE WEARING THAT HAT, CHIEF McGINNIS!
VERY FUNNY, BUT SHE INSISTED! SHE DOESN'T WANT ANYTHING RUINING NOSTALGIA WEEK!

MUCH AS I AGREED WITH CHIEF McGINNIS, THAT STILL DIDN'T EXPLAIN THE **DOLLHOUSE**. IT'D BEEN MOVED INSIDE THE CITY HALL TO PROTECT IT FROM THE WEATHER.
HMM... EVERYONE WE ASKED SAID THE DOLLS WERE IN A **DIFFERENT** POSITION BEFORE THE UNVEILING! AND THE CASE WAS **LOCKED** THE WHOLE TIME!
WHAT KIND OF GHOST WOULD HAUNT A DOLLHOUSE, ANYWAY?
A LITTLE **TINY** GHOST?
MAKE FUN IF YOU LIKE, BUT THIS IS REALLY **CREEPING** ME OUT!
I HAVE A STUFFED MONKEY IN MY ROOM, A SOUVENIR FROM MY TRIP TO **LILAC INN** LAST SUMMER – AND NOW I CAN'T GET TO SLEEP BECAUSE I THINK IT'S **STARING** AT ME!
MAYBE YOU SHOULD COVER IT WITH A BLANKET.
BUT I'M AFRAID IT'LL **SUFFO-CATE**!
HEY! THAT SECURITY CAMERA WOULD SHOW WHATEVER HAPPENED TO THE DOLLHOUSE!

YEAH, CHIEF McGINNIS ALREADY ASKED ABOUT IT! SORRY, BUT THAT CAMERA'S ON THE *FRITZ*!
OH WELL, I KIND OF FIGURED I SHOULD TRY TO SOLVE THIS CASE **WITHOUT** MODERN TECHNOLOGY, ANYWAY, IN KEEPING WITH THE... UH... ***SPIRIT*** OF NOSTALGIA WEEK!

OH MY GOSH! OH MY GOSH!
LOOK!
I TURNED MY BACK FOR A ***SECOND*** AND THE DOLLS ***CHANGED***! I DIDN'T EVEN SEE THAT ***TREE*** BEFORE!
IT LOOKS LIKE THAT ONE IS STEALING A ***HORSE***!

NOT ONLY THAT, BUT THE TOY TREE LOOKED JUST LIKE A PRETTY FAMOUS TREE RIGHT OUTSIDE RIVER HEIGHTS.
LEGEND HAD IT, THE RACKHAM GANG HAD A SHOOTOUT WITH A LOCAL FARMER HERE OVER A CENTURY AGO.
STRANGE SCENE FOR A NEW CRIME, BUT PERFECT FOR A PICNIC WITH MY BOYFRIEND, NED NICKERSON. AND AFTER TWO HOURS, NOT A HORSE IN SIGHT!
IT SAYS HERE SPIRITUALISM WAS BIG IN THE 1930s. PEOPLE USED EVERY-THING FROM AUTOMATIC WRITING TO TIPPING TABLES TO TALK TO THE DEAD!
YEAH, WELL, THE FAMOUS MAGICIAN HARRY HOUDINI SPENT A LOT OF HIS LIFE DEBUNKING THAT STUFF!
HE SWORE IF THERE WERE AN AFTERLIFE THAT HE'D COME BACK, AND WE'RE STILL WAITING!
MAYBE, BUT YOU HAVE TO ADMIT THERE ARE PROBABLY THINGS IN THE WORLD EVEN YOU CAN'T EXPLAIN!
NANCE?
NED WAS RIGHT, THERE WERE LOTS OF THINGS I COULDN'T EXPLAIN. AND RIGHT THEN, I WAS STARING AT ONE!

I DON'T BELIEVE IT! IT'S JUST LIKE THE DOLL HOUSE!
NOW THAT'S QUITE A COINCIDENCE!

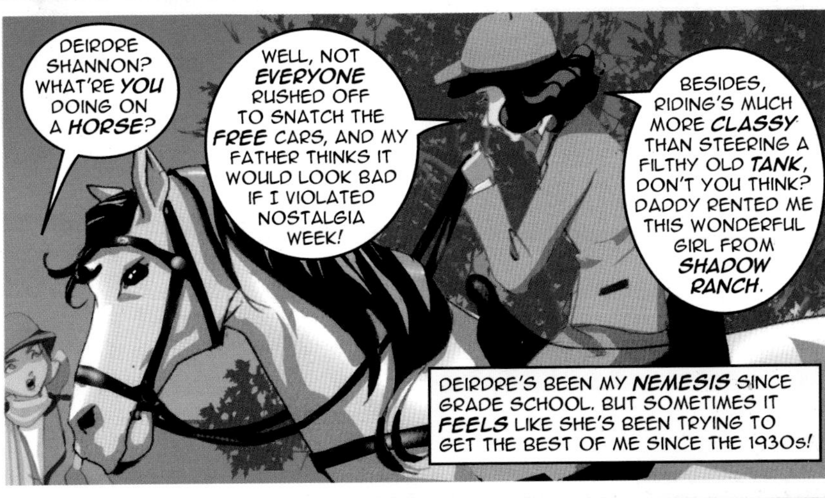
DEIRDRE SHANNON? WHAT'RE YOU DOING ON A HORSE?
WELL, NOT EVERYONE RUSHED OFF TO SNATCH THE FREE CARS, AND MY FATHER THINKS IT WOULD LOOK BAD IF I VIOLATED NOSTALGIA WEEK!
BESIDES, RIDING'S MUCH MORE CLASSY THAN STEERING A FILTHY OLD TANK, DON'T YOU THINK? DADDY RENTED ME THIS WONDERFUL GIRL FROM SHADOW RANCH.
DEIRDRE'S BEEN MY NEMESIS SINCE GRADE SCHOOL. BUT SOMETIMES IT FEELS LIKE SHE'S BEEN TRYING TO GET THE BEST OF ME SINCE THE 1930s!

TO MAKE THINGS WORSE, SHE'S ALWAYS TRYING TO FLIRT WITH MY BOYFRIEND!
NED, YOU SURE ARE THE BEE'S FLEAS IN THAT OUTFIT!
IF YOU MEAN THE OLD SLANG TERM, I THINK YOU MEAN BEE'S KNEES! BUT THANKS, I THINK...

LOOK, DIERDRE, THE FIGURES IN MADAME BLAVATSKY'S DOLLHOUSE AT THE TOWN CENTER SHOWED SOMEONE STEALING A **HORSE** RIGHT BY THIS TREE.
THE **LAST** CRIME IT SHOWED CAME TRUE! SO... I KNOW IT SOUNDS **WEIRD**, BUT I THINK YOU SHOULD BE **CAREFUL**!
SOUNDS WEIRD?! HMM... NOW WHY WOULD IT **SOUND** WEIRD?
OH, I KNOW! THAT'S BECAUSE IT **IS** WEIRD! **TOTALLY** WEIRD! JUST LIKE THOSE **CLOTHES** YOU HAVE ON!
OH DEAR! I'D BETTER GET HOME AND CONSULT MY **MONOPOLY** BOARD TO PROTECT MYSELF!

SO NED, WANT TO COME WITH?
I THINK YOU MEANT **OUIJA** BOARD, AND, NO THANKS!

HAVE IT YOUR WAY! GUESS I'D BETTER GET OUT OF HERE BEFORE SOME HORSE THIEVES SHOW UP!
HA! THAT'S MORE WILD WEST THAN 1930s ANYWAY!
UH... DEIRDRE?

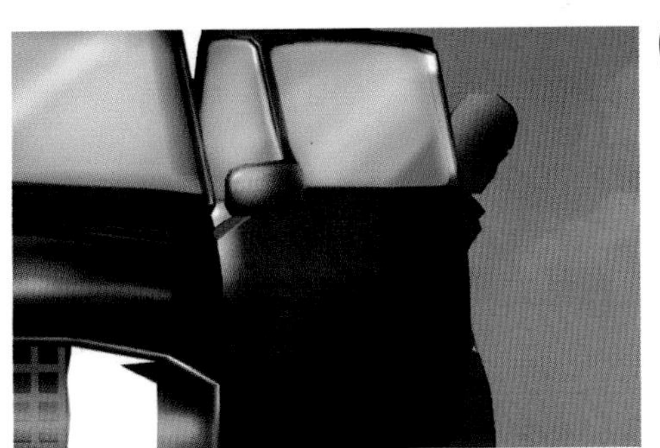

LOOK OUT!

NED, HELP!!

WHOA! EASY THERE!
DISTRACT HIM! I'LL GET THE HORSE!

DISTRACT HIM?
LIKE THIS?
WOK

I FIGURED THERE MUST BE SOMETHING SPECIAL ABOUT THE HORSE IF THE CROOK WANTED IT SO BADLY!

AND I WASN'T ABOUT TO LET A BIG CLUE LIKE THAT SLIP AWAY!

UNFORTUNATELY, THOUGH NED'S PRETTY STRONG, THE CROOK SLIPPED AWAY FROM HIM!
AND I HAD A FEELING AN APPLE WASN'T GOING TO STOP HIM THIS TIME!!

ESPECIALLY WHEN HE HAD A TRUCK!
OF COURSE IN KEEPING WITH NOSTALGIA WEEK, I DIDN'T BRING MY CELL! AND THE CLOSEST PLACE TO GO FOR HELP WAS RED GATE FARM, FIVE MILES AWAY!
NED HOPPED IN MY ROADSTER TO HELP, BUT IT WASN'T MADE FOR OFF-ROAD DRIVING!

NOT ONLY WAS THE CHASE OFF-ROAD, BUT SOON, I WAS OFF-HORSE!

UNLIKE DEIRDRE, I WASN'T EXACTLY ***DRESSED*** FOR RIDING, Y'KNOW.

MY HEAD HIT SOME-THING, ***HARD.***

I FELT GRASS UNDER ME, THEN EVERYTHING STARTED GOING FUZZY.

THE LAST THING I REMEMBERED WAS THE CROOK TAKING THE HORSE BACK TOWARD HIS TRUCK.

THEN FOR THE LONGEST TIME ***NOTHING***.

NEXT THING I KNEW, I WAS IN A BALLROOM. EVERYONE I KNEW WAS THERE, ONLY THEY ALL WORE OLD STYLE CLOTHES. IT WAS SOME KIND OF PARTY.
NED AND I WHIRLED ACROSS THE FLOOR.
SO I KNEW IT WAS A DREAM. I LOVE NED, HE'S GREAT, BUT HE'S NOT MUCH OF A DANCER.
THEN HE SAID SOMETHING TERRIBLY FUNNY, OR I GUESS HE DID, BECAUSE WE WERE BOTH LAUGHING.
IT WAS THE PERFECT EVENING, THE PERFECT DATE, THE PERFECT DREAM...

ONLY, IT TURNS OUT, IT WASN'T A DREAM.
IT WAS A NIGHTMARE!
NOW DO YOU BELIEVE SPIRITS HAUNT MY DOLLHOUSE?

YEOW!

WELCOME BACK TO THE WORLD OF THE LIVING!
TO ANSWER YOUR FIRST QUESTION, NED IS *FINE*. HE'S DOWNSTAIRS, WAITING.
TO ANSWER YOUR *NEXT* TWO QUESTIONS, NO, THEY *DIDN'T* CATCH THE CROOK AND YOU'VE BEEN *OUT* FOR ABOUT THREE HOURS.

HANNAH'S BEEN OUR HOUSEKEEPER EVER SINCE MOM DIED WHEN I WAS LITTLE. SOMETIMES I THINK SHE KNOWS ME BETTER THAN I KNOW *MYSELF*.
AND THE DOCTOR SAYS YOU'LL BE *FINE*, TOO. DID I LEAVE ANYTHING *OUT*?
NOPE! I GUESS THAT *COVERS* IT!

HEIGH
FORTUNATELY, THE ROADSTER WAS NONE THE WORSE FOR WEAR, AND AFTER I DROPPED NED OFF AT HOME, I WENT TO VISIT CHIEF McGINNIS.
SINCE HE'D INVITED ME INTO THE CRIME SCENE, I THOUGHT HE MIGHT STILL BE WILLING TO SHARE INFORMATION.
I WAS WRONG.

LOOK AT THAT BUMP ON YOUR HEAD. YOU'VE ALREADY BEEN HURT! AND YOUR BOYFRIEND NED'S LUCKY HE'S IN ONE PIECE!
I'D BE CRAZY TO GIVE YOU ANY MORE INFORMATION ON THIS CASE!
BUT YOU ARE GOING TO HAVE SOMEONE WATCH THE DOLLHOUSE, RIGHT?

SURE, AND MAYBE I'LL SET UP A GHOST DETECTOR, AS WELL!
YOU'RE A SMART GIRL, NANCY! SURELY YOU KNOW WHAT A COINCIDENCE IS! THERE'S NO EVIDENCE THESE CRIMES ARE LINKED.

TECHNICALLY, HE WAS RIGHT I SUPPOSE, BUT I HAD A *HUNCH*, AND MY HUNCHES ARE SELDOM WRONG.
SO, IF CHIEF McGINNIS WASN'T GOING TO DO A STAKEOUT ON THE DOLLHOUSE...

THEN *I* WOULD.
SOMEONE HAD TO BE MOVING THOSE DOLLS AROUND, AND TO FIND OUT WHO, I DECIDED TO DO IT THE OLD FASHIONED WAY...
BY SITTING AND *WATCHING*.

UNFORTUNATELY, THIS MEANS A LITTLE *BREAKING AND ENTERING*, BUT IT WAS FOR A GOOD CAUSE.

BESS AND GEORGE THINK THAT WHEN I HAVE MY HEAD IN A *MYSTERY*, I FORGET EVERYTHING ELSE - GAS, APPOINTMENTS...

THEY EVEN THINK I FORGET TO BE *SCARED*.
THEY'RE WRONG ABOUT THAT PART. I CERTAINLY *DO* GET SCARED, PARTICULARLY WHEN I'M ALL ALONE AT NIGHT IN A HUGE BUILDING.

FOCUSING HELPS, THINKING ABOUT THE PROBLEM. THEN, BEFORE YOU KNOW IT...

HOURS PASS.

FINALLY, AT ABOUT *THREE* IN THE MORNING, I HEARD SOMETHING.
A QUICK SHINE OF THE FLASHLIGHT SHOWED A MOVING SHADOW.
SKRCH
SKRCH

I *KNOW* IT WAS RIDICULOUS, BUT PART OF ME WAS HALF-EXPECTING TO SEE ONE OF MRS. BLAVATSKY'S *SPIRITS*.

I SHOOK THE THOUGHT OUT OF MY HEAD, AND TRIED TO FOCUS, TO *QUIET* MY BEATING HEART.

SKRCH

SKRCH

BUT *NOTHING* COULD HAVE PREPARED ME FOR WHAT I SAW...
SKRCH
SKRCH

THE DOLLS WERE MOVING BY THEMSELVES!
END CHAPTER ONE

I'D LIKE TO SAY I WASN'T SCARED, BUT COME ON, THE DOLLS WERE MOVING!
I MEAN, I'M USUALLY PRETTY GOOD ABOUT THIS KIND OF THING, BUT YES, I WAS OFFICIALLY FREAKED.
I WANTED TO RUN, BUT MY FEET WOULDN'T COOPERATE.
IN A WAY, IT MAY HAVE BEEN LUCKY I FELL, BECAUSE BY THE TIME I GOT BACK UP, I'D GOTTEN A HOLD OF MYSELF.
OOPS!
I REALIZED THAT SINCE IT COULDN'T BE SPIRITS, IT MUST BE SOME SORT OF TRICK, AND I WAS DETERMINED TO FIND OUT WHAT KIND OF TRICK IT WAS!
CHAPTER TWO: GHOST OF A CLUE

BUT BEFORE I COULD GET BACK TO THE DOLLHOUSE...
SOMEONE IN THERE?
MR. DUNCAN, THE WATCHMAN, LOOKED SO MUCH LIKE HE'D STEPPED FROM THE PAST, IT WAS HARD NOT TO SMILE.
DON'T BE LOOKING AT ME FUNNY, NANCY DREW, I'M NOT THE ONE TRES-PASSING!
MAYOR STRONG ASKED ME TO WEAR THIS GET-UP FOR NOSTALGIA WEEK! WHAT'S YOUR EXCUSE?
WHEN I EXPLAINED HE HURRIED OVER TO THE HOUSE.
DAGNAB IT! CHIEF McGINNIS TOLD ME TO KEEP AN EYE OUT. NOW I'VE MISSED THE WHOLE THING!
THE DOLLS REALLY DID CHANGE! THIS IS ONE FOR THE OL' DIARY! IF I HAD A CLUE WHERE I PUT IT, THAT IS!

MR. DUNCAN, DID YOU SEE THIS DOLLHOUSE SET UP? COULD THE DOLLS BE MECHANICAL? WAS THERE ANY MACHINERY?
DON'T THINK SO. I THINK IT WAS SOLID.
EXCUSE ME.
SURE THING.
I FIGURED THERE WAS ONLY ONE WAY TO SOLVE THIS MYSTERY FOR SURE!
HEY! THAT'S PRIVATE PROPERTY!

MRS. BLAVATSKY WOULD SCREAM BLOODY MURDER IF YOU SMASHED HER OLD DOLL-HOUSE!
ACTUALLY, I WAS JUST AIMING TO CRACK THE CASE, BUT HE WAS RIGHT. SOMETIMES I JUST GET SO FOCUSED ON A MYSTERY, I FORGET MYSELF A LITTLE.
WHAT'S THAT?
THE POLICE. I CALLED SOON AS I HEARD SOMETHING MOVING IN HERE, JUST LIKE I WAS SUPPOSED TO!
GREAT. I FIGURED I'D BE ARRESTED FOR TRESPASSING! I WONDERED WHAT 1930s PRISONS LOOKED LIKE.
AS IT TURNED OUT, CHIEF McGINNIS WASN'T AS ANGRY AS I EXPECTED. BUT HE DIDN'T EXACTLY BELIEVE ME, EITHER.
IT'S LATE, YOU'RE TIRED AND YOU HAD THAT BUMP ON YOUR HEAD. SURE YOU JUST DIDN'T IMAGINE IT?
TELL YOU THE TRUTH, NANCY, I WANTED TO CRACK OPEN THAT CASE MYSELF AFTER THE HORSE THEFT.
BUT MRS. BLAVATSKY REFUSED. I EVEN TRIED TO CONVINCE JUDGE WATERS TO GIVE ME A WARRANT, BUT HE DOESN'T LOOK KINDLY ON GHOST STORIES!
AND WITH THAT NEW DEAD END, IT WAS TIME FOR THIS GIRL DETECTIVE TO GET SOME SLEEP.

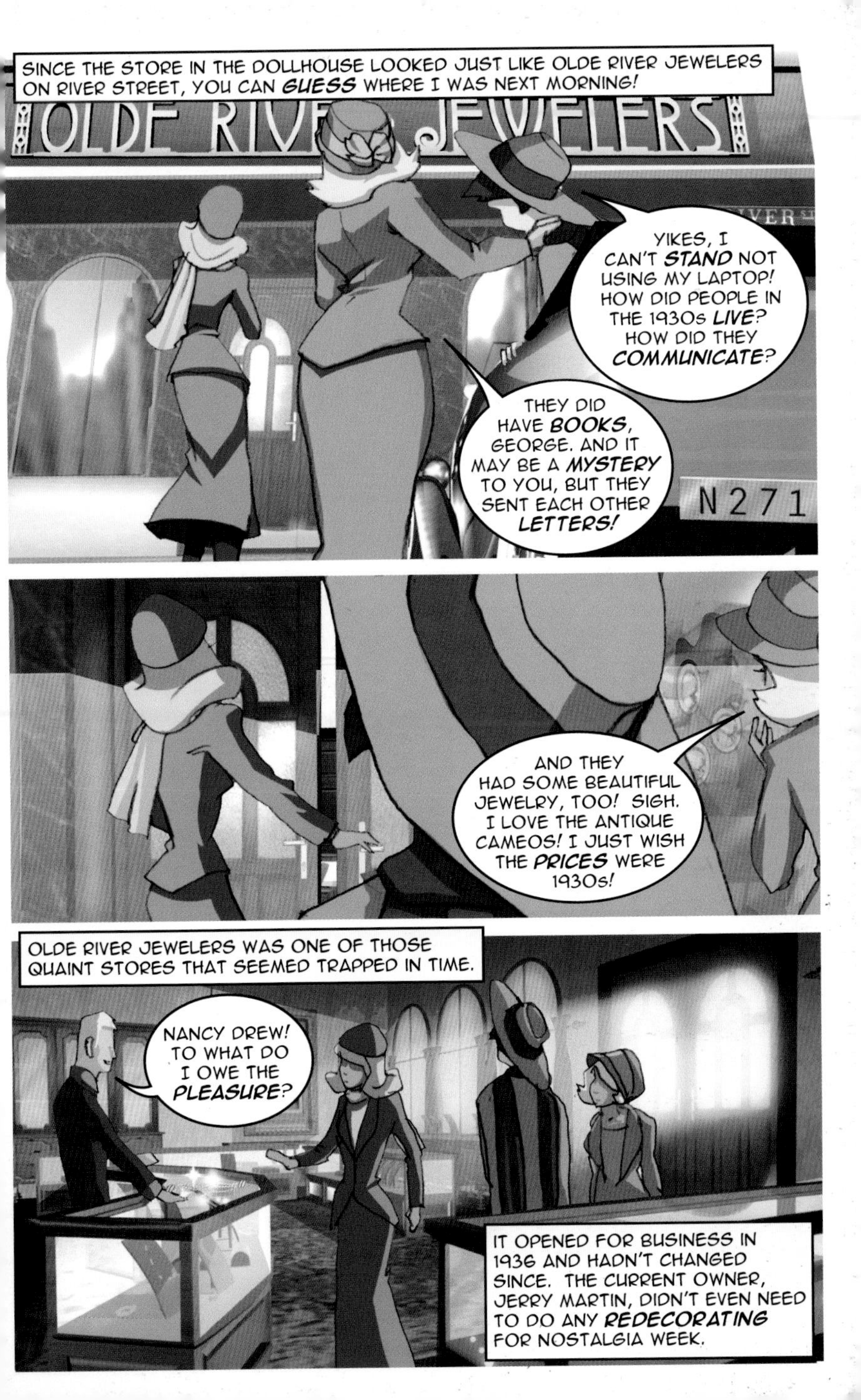
SINCE THE STORE IN THE DOLLHOUSE LOOKED JUST LIKE OLDE RIVER JEWELERS ON RIVER STREET, YOU CAN GUESS WHERE I WAS NEXT MORNING!
OLDE RIVER JEWELERS
YIKES, I CAN'T STAND NOT USING MY LAPTOP! HOW DID PEOPLE IN THE 1930s LIVE? HOW DID THEY COMMUNICATE?
THEY DID HAVE BOOKS, GEORGE. AND IT MAY BE A MYSTERY TO YOU, BUT THEY SENT EACH OTHER LETTERS!
N 271
AND THEY HAD SOME BEAUTIFUL JEWELRY, TOO! SIGH. I LOVE THE ANTIQUE CAMEOS! I JUST WISH THE PRICES WERE 1930s!
OLDE RIVER JEWELERS WAS ONE OF THOSE QUAINT STORES THAT SEEMED TRAPPED IN TIME.
NANCY DREW! TO WHAT DO I OWE THE PLEASURE?
IT OPENED FOR BUSINESS IN 1936 AND HADN'T CHANGED SINCE. THE CURRENT OWNER, JERRY MARTIN, DIDN'T EVEN NEED TO DO ANY REDECORATING FOR NOSTALGIA WEEK.

I FEEL A LITTLE SILLY SAYING THIS, BUT DID CHIEF McGINNIS TELL YOU ABOUT THE UH... DOLLHOUSE, MR. MARTIN?
THAT HE DID! HE'S STOPPING BY HIMSELF EVERY HOUR. NOSTALGIA WEEK HAS THE RIVER HEIGHTS POLICE DEPARTMENT STRETCHED PRETTY THIN, I GUESS.

YOU'RE NOT WORRIED?
ABOUT A HAUNTED DOLLHOUSE? I THOUGHT IT WAS PRETTY FUNNY!

THAT KIND OF STUFF MAY HAVE BEEN SPOOKY A LONG TIME AGO! BUT, THIS ISN'T REALLY THE 1930s!
I MEAN, DO YOU EXPECT ME TO BELIEVE SOMEONE WITH A MASK WILL JUST WALK IN HERE AND SAY...

STICK 'EM UP!
EEP!

PLEASE JUST TAKE WHATEVER YOU WANT.

OKAY! THAT NECKLACE WILL DO NICELY!

AND DON'T GET ANY FUNNY IDEAS ABOUT FOLLOWING ME, ESPECIALLY YOU, NANCY DREW!
THE SPIRITS WOULDN'T LIKE THAT!

WHOA, GIRL! YOU STAY RIGHT HERE!
I'M NOT AFRAID OF ANY SPIRITS!
FORGET THE SPIRITS, DIDN'T YOU SEE THE GUN?

THEY MADE ME COUNT TO TEN, THEN AGREED TO LET ME SEE IF I COULD FIGURE OUT WHICH DIRECTION HE RAN IN.
HE VANISHED! LIKE A... GHOST!
NO, LIKE SOME-ONE WITH A CAR.
THOSE TIRE TRACKS ARE FRESH.
I THOUGHT ABOUT FOLLOWING WITH MY CAR, BUT THE CROOK WAS LONG GONE.
STRANGER STILL, I SOON LEARNED THAT THE STOLEN NECKLACE WAS FAKE! MR. MARTIN JUST USED IT FOR DISPLAY!

DID YOU KNOW IN 1924, AMERICANS CONSUMED LESS THAN 4 QUARTS OF ICE CREAM A YEAR? TODAY, IT'S LIKE 15 QUARTS.
THAT WAS THE LAST THING I READ ON THE INTERNET. I MISS IT SO MUCH!
THIS IS A TOUGH ONE! WHAT MADE THOSE DOLLS MOVE? AND WHY STEAL A FAKE PAINTING... A FAKE NECKLACE?

MAYBE SINCE THE SPIRIT DOLLS ARE LITTLE FAKE PEOPLE, THEY LIKE FAKE STUFF!
WILL YOU STOP WITH THE SPIRIT STUFF, BESS? DEIRDRE'S HORSE WAS REAL. AT LEAST IT LOOKED REAL.
OW! YOU'RE MEAN IN THE 1930s!
OH, SHE'S JUST GRUMPY WITHOUT HER MODERN CON-VENIENCES.
THE HORSE WAS REAL, JUST NOT VALUABLE! MAYBE THAT'S THE POINT. MAYBE THE CROOK ISN'T STEALING STUFF TO MAKE MONEY.
WHY ELSE WOULD SOMEONE STEAL? IT'S A LOUSY WAY TO GET FAMOUS!

TROUBLE GETTING THAT BIG BRAIN OF YOURS TO WORK, NANCY? ISN'T IT OBVIOUS GHOSTS ARE FOR REAL?
EW! I AGREE WITH DEIRDRE! EW! EW!
AND I SHOULD KNOW! I SAW ONE! WELL... ALMOST!
I WAS ON A DATE WITH DAN FREEDMAN JUST LAST SUMMER, ENJOYING A VERY ROMANTIC EVENING.
ALL AT ONCE, HE TURNED AND RAN! HE SAID HE ACTUALLY SAW A GHOST FLYING IN THE WOODS!
EVER THINK MAYBE DAN WAS JUST TRYING TO GET AWAY FROM YOU?
LAUGH IF YOU WANT, BUT I WOULDN'T MESS WITH GHOSTS, NANCY DREW! EVEN LITTLE ONES!

LEFT TO MYSELF, I WOULD HAVE SPENT THE REST OF NOSTALGIA WEEK JUST THINKING ABOUT THAT DOLLHOUSE!
AS IT WAS, BESS AND GEORGE DRAGGED ME TO A BIG PARTY THAT NIGHT ON THE FAMOUS OLD STEAMBOAT THE MAGNOLIA BELLE.
STEAMBOATS ACTUALLY GO ALL THE WAY BACK TO 1769, BUT THEY DIDN'T MAKE MUCH MONEY UNTIL ROBERT FULTON STARTED BUILDING THEM IN 1801.
TECHNICALLY THE MAGNOLIA BELLE WAS A LOT OLDER THAN 1930, BUT IT WAS LAST FIXED UP IN 1935, SO IT FIT RIGHT IN!
GOOD THING, TOO - SHE WAS A GLORIOUS OLD SHIP!

EVEN MY DAD, CARSON DREW, WAS THERE, DOING THE *LINDY* WITH MRS. MAHONEY. HE'S A GREAT LAWYER, AND NOT A BAD DANCER!
THE "LINDY HOP" WAS NAMED AFTER CHARLES LINDBERGH, THE FIRST MAN TO "HOP" ACROSS THE ATLANTIC OCEAN IN A SOLO FLIGHT IN 1927. THE DANCE WAS A HUGE CRAZE BY THE 1930s.
SHALL WE CUT A RUG? THAT'S OLD SLANG FOR...
I KNOW, NED, FOR *DANCING*. SURE!
FUNNY, BUT LINDBERGH NEVER DANCED HIMSELF. AND BY THE LATE 1930S, THE NAME OF THE DANCE CHANGED TO THE *JITTERBUG* ANYWAY!
WHATEVER THE *NAME*, IT SURE WAS A LOT OF *FUN*!

I WAS HAVING A GREAT TIME, BUT MY MIND KEPT DRIFTING BACK TO OTHER THINGS.
THINGS LIKE, WAS I WRONG? WAS I BEING TOO SKEPTICAL ABOUT THE SPIRIT WORLD?
THERE WAS A KIND OF MAGIC FEELING IN THE AIR AS WE REACHED OUT TO THE PAST.
SO, WAS IT IMPOSSIBLE TO THINK THAT THE PAST COULD ALSO BE REACHING OUT TO US?
YOU KNOW, BACK IN THE REAL 1930s, THERE PROBABLY WEREN'T ANY GIRL DETECTIVES!
EMMA BLAVATSKY!

ACTUALLY, ANNE RODWAY SOLVED THE MURDER OF HER BEST FRIEND BACK IN 1859. I THINK SHE WAS THE FIRST.
MRS. BLAVATSKY, IF YOU DON'T MIND MY ASKING, WHY WON'T YOU LET US OPEN THE DOLLHOUSE? DO YOU HAVE SOMETHING TO HIDE?
HIDE? AT MY AGE, THERE IS LITTLE TO HIDE.
I DON'T WISH THE HOUSE DISTURBED, BECAUSE IT WOULD DISTURB THE SPIRITS! THEY HAVE SO MUCH TO TELL US.
THEY SURE HAVE AN ODD WAY OF TALKING! PREDICTING THE THEFT OF WORTHLESS THINGS?
YOU DOUBT, BUT WHAT IF YOUR CLUES LED TO PROOF THAT THE SPIRIT WORLD REALLY DOES EXIST?
PROOF? WELL, I GUESS I'D BE PRETTY FAMOUS THEN, WOULDN'T I?
WHY DON'T YOU COME TO MY HOME TOMORROW, AND TOGETHER WE CAN TRY TO CONTACT THEM?
WHO KNOWS? PERHAPS WE WILL BOTH BE FAMOUS.

I CAN'T BELIEVE I LET YOU GUYS TALK ME INTO A SEANCE!
COME ON, YOU KNOW YOU'RE DYING TO SEE A GHOSTY!
IT'S THE DYING PART THAT SCARES ME!
YOU'RE ALL HERE. EXCELLENT. LET'S GET STARTED!
IN THERE? IN THE DARK?

THE SPIRITS PREFER THE DARK, MY DEAR. THEIR DAYS IN THE LIGHT ARE OVER, AND IT MAKES THEM FEEL AT HOME.
DARKNESS ALSO MAKES IT EASIER TO FOOL PEOPLE!
I KIND OF KNEW WHAT TO EXPECT.
PLEASE. BE SEATED.
SEE, AFTER THE DANCE, NED LOANED ME THE BOOK HE WAS READING ABOUT SPIRITUALISM.

, TOO, HAVE ED.
THIS TWISTED CANDLE HAS BEEN SPECIALLY BLESSED TO ATTRACT SPIRITS!
BUT AS IT TURNED OUT, EMMA BLAVATSKY WENT TOTALLY BY THE BOOK!
LET US JOIN TOGETHER IN A CIRCLE, AND LET THIS CIRCLE REMAIN UNBROKEN.
AVATSKY, S OUR A FEW OKE
AR ME, S OF THE ED! I KNOW LK AMONG NOW YOU H US AND VE TO PEAK!
PLEASE TELL US! TELL US WHAT YOU WANT US TO KNOW!

THEN, ALL AT ONCE, I FELT LIKE MY HAND WAS BEING SQUEEZED IN A VISE!
THEN I REALIZED IT WAS BESS! THE POOR DEAR WAS SO SCARED SHE WAS CRUSHING MY HAND.
RELAX. IT HASN'T EVEN STARTED YET.
Y-YES IT HAS, N-N-NANCE! LOOK!

EVEN THIS PART WAS IN THE BOOK.
SPIRITUALISTS CLAIMED THESE GHOSTLY FORMS WERE MADE FROM SOMETHING CALLED ECTOPLASM.
BUT IT WAS REALLY USUALLY MUSLIN, A CHEAP FABRIC THAT COULD BE ROLLED UP AND EASILY HIDDEN.
PRETTY IMPRESSIVE, THOUGH, HUH?

OHHHHHH!
AT THE HEIGHT OF THE SEANCE, THE SPIRIT WOULD ALWAYS FIND SOME WAY TO COMMUNICATE.
SOMETIMES THEY TAPPED OUT ANSWERS TO QUESTIONS BY TIPPING THE TABLE.
SOMETIMES THEY MOVED A PEN IN THE HAND OF THE MEDIUM TO WRITE A MESSAGE.
AND SOMETIMES, THEY USED THE MOUTH OF THE MEDIUM TO JUST, WELL... TALK!
OHHHHHH!
DO NOT DOUBT US NANCY DREW! TELL THE WORLD WE ARE REAL!
OR YOU WILL BECOME A VICTIM OF OUR CURSE!
AND, OF COURSE, AT THE VERY END, THE CANDLE ALWAYS GETS MYSTERIOUSLY BLOWN OUT!
WHOOSH

THEN THE MEDIUM WAKES UP AND ACTS LIKE NOTHING HAPPENED!
MY, MY!
THE REALLY AMAZING THING IS HOW MANY PEOPLE BELIEVED THIS STUFF!
I MUST HAVE PASSED OUT FROM THE EXCITEMENT!
SO, DID ANYTHING HAPPEN? DID THE SPIRITS SPEAK?
DID ANYTHING HAPPEN?!
DID ANYTHING HAPPEN?!
THERE WAS A BIG GHOST AND... AND...A WEIRD VOICE AND IT THREATENED NANCY!

BESS, THERE'S A BOOK YOU'VE REALLY GOT TO READ! IT EXPLAINS HOW ALL THESE SEANCES ARE FAKED.
FAKED?
YEAH, LIKE NOT REAL! SOME PEOPLE PAY A MINT TO SPEAK TO THEIR DEAD LOVED ONES! GEE, FOR A MECHANICAL GENIUS, YOU SURE CAN BE GULLIBLE!

GEORGE IS A LITTLE CRANKY, BUT SHE'S RIGHT.
THEY USED ALL KINDS OF TRICKS, LIKE WIRES, FOLDS IN THEIR CLOTHING, HOLLOW SPACES IN THE TABLE

WAIT A MINUTE.

EEEP!
HOLLOW SPACE? OF COURSE!

ALL THIS TIME I'VE BEEN WONDERING HOW THOSE DOLLS MOVED BY THEM-SELVES!
I'VE BEEN THINKING MAYBE THEY WERE ROBOTS, REMOTE CONTROLLED OR SOMETHING!

IT JUST DAWNED ON ME, THE BASE COULD BE HOLLOW!
SOMEONE COULD HAVE BEEN HIDING INSIDE!

BUT THAT DOESN'T EXPLAIN HOW THE DOLLS *MOVED!*
NO, BUT *MAGNETS* WOULD!

IF THERE WERE *MAGNETS* IN THE DOLLS, SOMEONE COULD MOVE THEM FROM BENEATH WITH *ANOTHER* MAGNET.
HMM... THIS ALL LOOKS *SOLID*.

WAIT! THERE'S SOMETHING WEDGED UNDER IT!

PUSH, GIRLS, PUSH!
UNGH! EASY FOR YOU TO SAY!
THIS IS HEAVY FOR A HAUNTED DOLLHOUSE.

OOOMF! GOT IT!

WHAT IS IT?
SOME KIND OF BROKEN LOCKET!

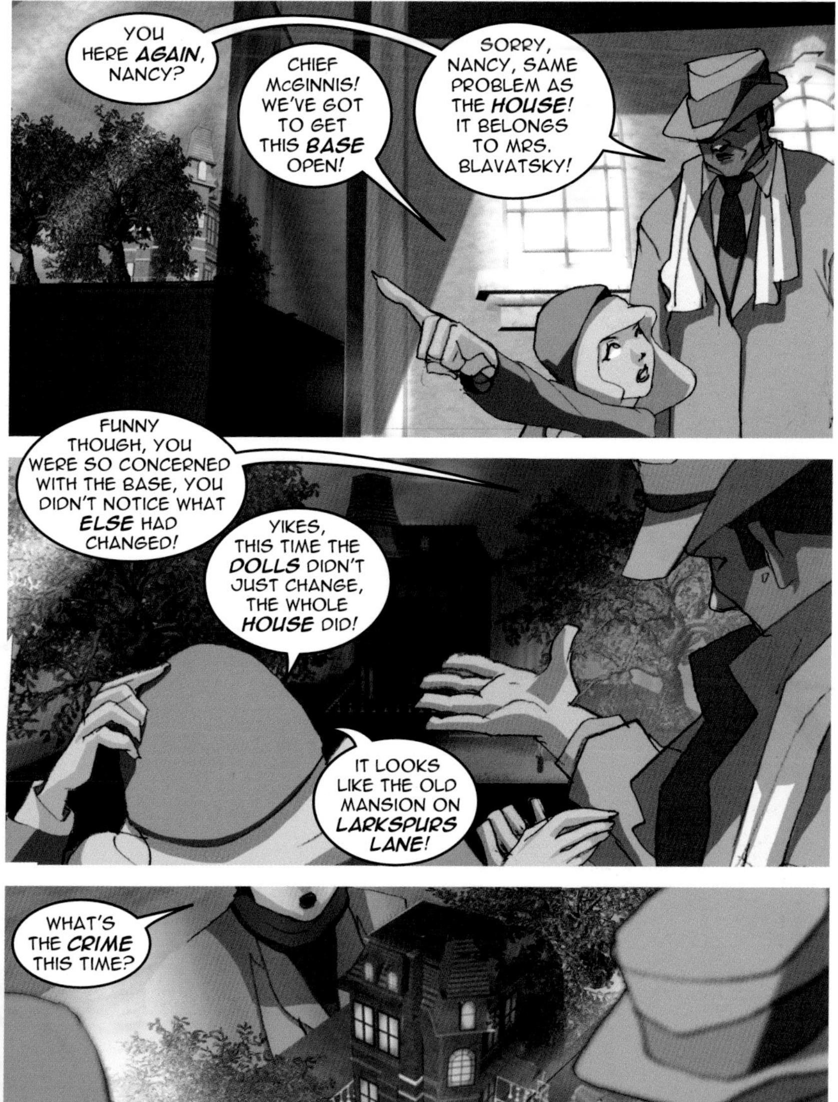
YOU HERE AGAIN, NANCY?
CHIEF McGINNIS! WE'VE GOT TO GET THIS BASE OPEN!
SORRY, NANCY, SAME PROBLEM AS THE HOUSE! IT BELONGS TO MRS. BLAVATSKY!
FUNNY THOUGH, YOU WERE SO CONCERNED WITH THE BASE, YOU DIDN'T NOTICE WHAT ELSE HAD CHANGED!
YIKES, THIS TIME THE DOLLS DIDN'T JUST CHANGE, THE WHOLE HOUSE DID!
IT LOOKS LIKE THE OLD MANSION ON LARKSPURS LANE!

WHAT'S THE CRIME THIS TIME?
MURDER.
THAT DOLL ON THE ROOF PUSHED THAT OTHER DOLL OFF.

NANCY, I HATE TO SAY IT, BUT THAT DOLL LYING THERE ON THE GROUND, KIND OF *DEAD*?
IT LOOKS LIKE *YOU*! IT'S EVEN GOT A LITTLE *LOCKET* IN ITS HAND!

AND THE CAR PARKED OUT FRONT LOOKS LIKE *YOURS*!
N2701
COME ON, HOW DO YOU KNOW IT'S NOT JUST *ANY* OLD BLUE ROADSTER?

ULP!
BECAUSE THE LICENSE *PLATE* IS THE *SAME* AS MINE!
N2701
END CHAPTER TWO

WON'T YOU PLEASE LET ME HELP LOOK FOR CLUES, CHIEF McGINNIS?
SORRY, BUT NO! CITY HALL IS OFFICIALLY CLOSED UNTIL WE GET TO THE BOTTOM OF THIS, AND I PROMISED YOUR FATHER I'D SEND YOU HOME!
WHATEVER YOU DO, DO NOT HEAD TO LARKSPUR LANE!
THAT PLACE IS FALLING APART! IT'S DANGEROUS WHETHER SOMETHING FISHY IS GOING ON OR NOT! LET THE POLICE HANDLE THINGS FOR A CHANGE!
CHAPTER THREE: NANCY GETS DOLLED UP
EEEP! I'M SO FREAKED OUT, I THOUGHT I HEARD THAT STATUE WHISPER!
THE ONLY WAY THAT STATUE COULD WHISPER IS IF SOMEONE WERE HIDING IN IT, THE SAME WAY SOMEONE MUST HAVE HIDDEN IN THE BASE OF THE DOLLHOUSE.
THE LOCKET WE FOUND PROVED THAT. I ONLY HOPED CHIEF McGINNIS WOULD GET A COURT ORDER NOW TO OPEN THE BASE!

IN ANY CASE, NOW THAT I WAS ONTO SOMETHING, I COULDN'T LET THIS MYSTERY GO, EVEN IF THE VICTIM COULD BE *ME*!
MAYBE WE SHOULD CHEAT A LITTLE ON ***NOSTALGIA WEEK*** AND DO SOME ***INTERNET*** RESEARCH ON HAUNTED DOLL-HOUSES BACK AT NANCY'S!

GET ***REAL***, BESS. WE'RE NOT GOING BACK TO NANCY'S. GET A LOAD OF THAT ***LOOK*** ON HER FACE!
NO?
NOPE.
WE'RE GOING TO THAT ***CREEPY*** HOUSE ON LARKSPUR LANE, AREN'T WE?
YUP.
NOTHING LIKE A ***GOOD*** FRIEND. THEY KNOW YOU SO WELL, SOMETIMES YOU ***BARELY*** HAVE TO TALK!
N2701

ABOUT 80 YEARS AGO, LARKSPUR LANE, JUST OUTSIDE OF TOWN, WAS WHERE THE RICHEST RIVER HEIGHTS CITIZENS OWNED WEEKEND HOMES.
THESE DAYS, IT WAS BARELY A ROAD!
HM! THAT KNOCKING CAN'T BE GOOD! COULD BE YOUR OIL, OR THE BEARINGS, OR IT COULD MEAN YOU'RE JUST...
KLUNK
KLUNK
...OUT OF GAS.
Y'KNOW, NANCE, I'M NOT EVEN MAD! I THINK IT'S PRETTY AMAZING YOU KEPT THE TANK FULL THIS LONG!

SIGH. ONLY BECAUSE HANNAH FILLED IT FOR ME, TWICE!
ANOTHER THING MY FRIENDS KNOW ABOUT ME IS SOMETIMES I GET SO WRAPPED-UP IN A CASE, I FORGET EVERYTHING ELSE!
AWW... I WAS JUST GETTING USED TO MY HYBRID, WHICH ONLY RAN OUT OF GAS EVERY OTHER WEEK!
OH, YOU DON'T HAVE TO BANG YOUR HEAD AGAINST THE STEERING WHEEL, SWEETIE!
LET HER, BESS. IT'LL SAVE ME THE TROUBLE.
AND OF COURSE WE DON'T HAVE OUR CELL PHONES! AFTER ALL, IT'S NOSTALGIA WEEK! WHOOP DEE DOO!
YOU REALLY HAVE TO WONDER HOW ANYONE SOLVED CRIMES BACK THEN!

I'D LIKE TO SAY THAT AT LEAST I REMEMBERED AN UMBRELLA, BUT HANNAH PACKED THAT, TOO!
I KNOW NOSTALGIA ISN'T YOUR THING, GEORGE, BUT HOW ABOUT CUTTING SOME SLACK FOR AN OLD FRIEND?

AW, DON'T LISTEN TO ME! I JUST MISS MY PC, MY PDA, MY LCD TV AND ALL THOSE OTHER BEAUTIFUL INITIALS.
PLUS, I'M COLD AND WE'RE WALKING TO A CREEPY HOUSE WHERE YOU MAY DIE.
BUT WHEREVER YOU GO NANCY, YOU KNOW I'LL BE THERE.

A CREEPY HOUSE WHERE I MAY DIE.
I KNEW GEORGE WAS SORT OF JOKING AROUND, BUT WHEN I SAW THE TOP OF THE MANSION STICK ITS HEAD ABOVE THE TREES, I FELT PRETTY SMALL AND SCARED.
AS IF I WERE A DOLL.

NOSTALGIA WEEK ASIDE, THE 1930s WERE NOT ALL FUN AND GAMES.
AFTER A HUGE STOCK MARKET CRASH IN 1929, *MILLIONS* OF PEOPLE WERE SUDDENLY *POOR* AND OUT OF WORK.
THAT'S WHY LARKSPUR LANE WAS *DESERTED*. IT WAS LIKE A *GHOST* OF WHAT WAS CALLED THE *GREAT DEPRESSION*.

LOOK! CHIEF McGINNIS HAS SOMEONE WATCHING THE PLACE! WE CAN GET A RIDE *HOME*!

NO! I'M *GLAD* HE'S THERE TOO, BUT *FIRST* I WANT TO TAKE A LOOK AROUND!
I'VE GOT A HUNCH THE *SOLUTION* TO THE MYSTERY IS IN THAT HOUSE, AND I'M NOT *LEAVING* YET!

OKAY, FINE! SO WE'LL GET A LITTLE MORE SOAKED. BUT HOW DO WE GET IN? THAT PLACE IS LOCKED UP!
MY DAD HAD A CLIENT WHO BOUGHT THE HOUSE LAST SUMMER, SO WE CAME OUT TO VISIT.

I HAPPEN TO KNOW A SET OF KEYS ARE HIDDEN...
INSIDE THIS HOLLOW OAK!
IF YOU CAN REMEMBER THAT, WHY NOT GAS?

THAT'S EASY. GAS ISN'T DIRECTLY RELATED TO THE CASE!
SHH! LET'S GO AROUND BACK TO KEEP OUT OF SIGHT OF THE SQUAD CAR!

WOW! TALK ABOUT ABANDONED! THEY EVEN TOOK THE KITCHEN SINK!
AT LEAST IT'S RAINING LESS INSIDE HERE.

ARE WE USING BATTERIES FROM THE 1930s, TOO? THE OLD FLASHLIGHTS ARE GOING DIM FAST!
I GUESS WE'RE LUCKY THEY'RE WORKING AT ALL!
OH, NANCY, WE'RE NOT LUCKY AT ALL! I MEAN, SHOULD WE EVEN BE HERE? GHOSTS OR NOT, THAT DOLLHOUSE SHOWED YOU DEAD!

RELAX, GEORGE! THIS ISN'T EXACTLY THE SAME AS THE DOLLHOUSE! THERE'S A POLICE CAR OUT FRONT, NOT THE ROADSTER! SO THINGS ARE ALREADY DIFFERENT!
SEE?

OOPS.
I SEE. BUT DO YOU SEE WHAT I SEE?

THE POLICE CAR IS GONE AND THE ROADSTER IS THERE!
JUST LIKE THE DOLL-HOUSE!

WE ARE SO OUT OF HERE!
WE'LL WALK BACK TO TOWN IF WE HAVE TO!

BRAVERY ISN'T ABOUT NOT BEING SCARED, IT'S ABOUT DOING THE RIGHT THING EVEN IF YOU ARE SCARED.
YOU GUYS DO WHAT YOU HAVE TO, BUT I'M CHECKING THIS HOUSE OUT.
I WAS SCARED, ALL RIGHT. I JUST HOPED I WAS DOING THE RIGHT THING!

OKAY, SO LET'S FOLLOW HER!
FINE, BUT... UM GEORGE, ARE YOU BREATHING HEAVY FROM THE RAIN?
NO. WHY?

EEP!
I HEARD SOME SHUFFLING BEHIND ME, SO I FIGURED BESS AND GEORGE WERE COMING ALONG.

I KNEW THEY WOULDN'T DESERT ME!
BUT THEY COULD BE SLOW POKES SOMETIMES.

ONCE, I'D SOLVED A WHOLE MYSTERY BY THE TIME IT TOOK THEM TO GET OUT OF THE CAR!
OF COURSE, OTHER TIMES, THEY'VE SAVED MY NECK, SO I WAS ALWAYS GLAD TO KNOW THEY WERE THERE.
OW! GET YOUR HAND OUT OF MY FACE PLEASE!
THAT'S NOT MY HAND, IT'S YOURS!

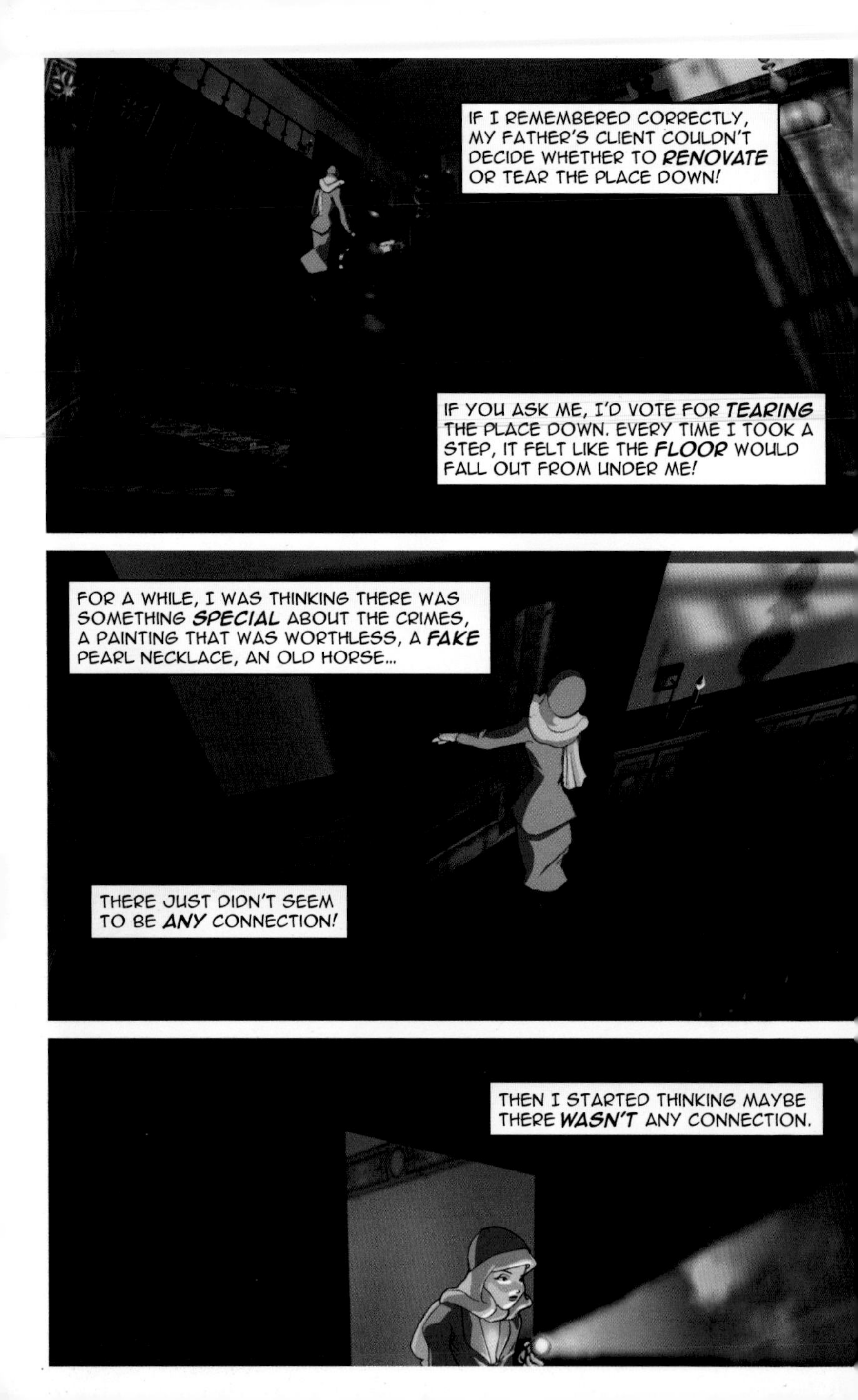
IF I REMEMBERED CORRECTLY, MY FATHER'S CLIENT COULDN'T DECIDE WHETHER TO *RENOVATE* OR TEAR THE PLACE DOWN!
IF YOU ASK ME, I'D VOTE FOR *TEARING* THE PLACE DOWN. EVERY TIME I TOOK A STEP, IT FELT LIKE THE *FLOOR* WOULD FALL OUT FROM UNDER ME!
FOR A WHILE, I WAS THINKING THERE WAS SOMETHING *SPECIAL* ABOUT THE CRIMES, A PAINTING THAT WAS WORTHLESS, A *FAKE* PEARL NECKLACE, AN OLD HORSE...
THERE JUST DIDN'T SEEM TO BE *ANY* CONNECTION!
THEN I STARTED THINKING MAYBE THERE *WASN'T* ANY CONNECTION.

BUT I HAD A FEELING THE LOOT WAS HERE.
AND I WAS *RIGHT*.

HERE WAS THE PORTRAIT AND THE NECKLACE.
ONLY, WHERE WAS THE *HORSE*?

WHINNNEYY!
OH. *THERE* IT WAS.

WHINNNEYY!
BETWEEN THE RAIN AND THE SHADOWS, THE HORSE LOOKED LIKE IT WAS HAUNTING A BRIDGE THAT CROSSED THE STREAM OUT BACK.

HAUNTED DOLLHOUSE, HAUNTED BRIDGE, I WAS STARTING TO FEEL LIKE I WAS IN SOME OLD 1930s MYSTERY BOOK!
IN FACT, IT WAS LIKE SOME-ONE WAS SETTING IT UP TO BE A MYSTERY! LIKE THEY USED A DOLL THAT LOOKED LIKE ME BECAUSE THEY KNEW I'D COME LOOK!

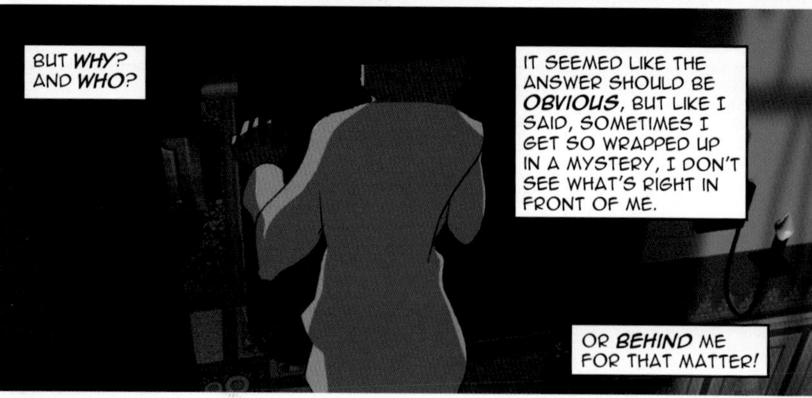
BUT WHY? AND WHO?
IT SEEMED LIKE THE ANSWER SHOULD BE OBVIOUS, BUT LIKE I SAID, SOMETIMES I GET SO WRAPPED UP IN A MYSTERY, I DON'T SEE WHAT'S RIGHT IN FRONT OF ME.
OR BEHIND ME FOR THAT MATTER!

I HEARD THE DOOR LOCK. I GUESS WHOEVER SHOVED US DOWN HERE MEANS TO KEEP US!
AT LEAST WE'RE NOT ALONE!

IT'S THE POLICE OFFICER FROM THE SQUAD CAR!
IS HE ALIVE?

OH, PLEASE, WAKE UP, MR. POLICE OFFICER! WE SURE COULD USE SOME HELP!
YES, HE'S JUST UNCON-SCIOUS!

ANYTHING WE CAN USE FOR A *PILLOW* TO MAKE HIM COMFORT-ABLE? LOOK AROUND!
I'M *ON* IT!
ANYTHING?
NOTHING! JUST THIS OLD *PHONE*! AND IT'S *DEAD* AND *USELESS*, WHICH IS JUST HOW I FEEL!

BESS, REMEMBER HOW I SAID WHOEVER SHOVED US IN HERE *LOCKED* US IN?
YEAH?
WELL IT LOOKS LIKE HE LOCKED US IN *WITH* HIM! YIKES!

BESS! HELP!
WHAM

HEY, I GUESS THAT PHONE WASN'T SO USELESS AFTER ALL!

NOW WHY WOULD SOMEONE GO THROUGH ALL THE TROUBLE OF LURING ME TO A CREEPY HOUSE? SURE, I WAS PRETTY WELL KNOWN FOR BEING A DETECTIVE...

OH. THE PIECES JUST FELL TOGETHER. IT WAS LIKE A SECRET PANEL OPENING IN MY HEAD.

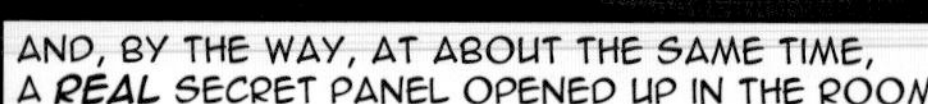

AND, BY THE WAY, AT ABOUT THE SAME TIME, A REAL SECRET PANEL OPENED UP IN THE ROOM.

BEYOND IT WAS A HIDDEN STAIRCASE, LEADING UP.

I WONDERED IF MY DAD'S CLIENT KNEW ABOUT ALL THE EXTRA FEATURES THE HOUSE HAD. MAYBE THERE WAS A DUNGEON SOMEWHERE, TOO.
ANYWAY, WHAT I FIGURED OUT WAS THAT SOMEONE MIGHT LEAD ME HERE BECAUSE I WAS KNOWN FOR BEING HOPELESSLY CURIOUS AND TRYING TO FIND THE TRUTH.
I'M ALSO PROUD TO SAY THAT I'M TRUSTWORTHY.

SO, IF SOMETHING HAPPENED TO ME, OR I STARTED TO BELIEVE IN THE HAUNTED DOLLHOUSE, LOTS OF OTHER PEOPLE WOULD, TOO.

SO THE QUESTION NOW WAS, WHO WOULD WANT EVERYONE TO BELIEVE IN A HAUNTED DOLLHOUSE?
WHOEVER IT WAS MADE SURE EVERYTHING HERE WOULD LOOK JUST LIKE THE SCENE BACK IN CITY HALL.THEY EVEN MADE SURE MY CAR WOULD BE HERE.
THERE WAS ONLY ONE THING MISSING.

THE PERSON WHO KILLS ME!

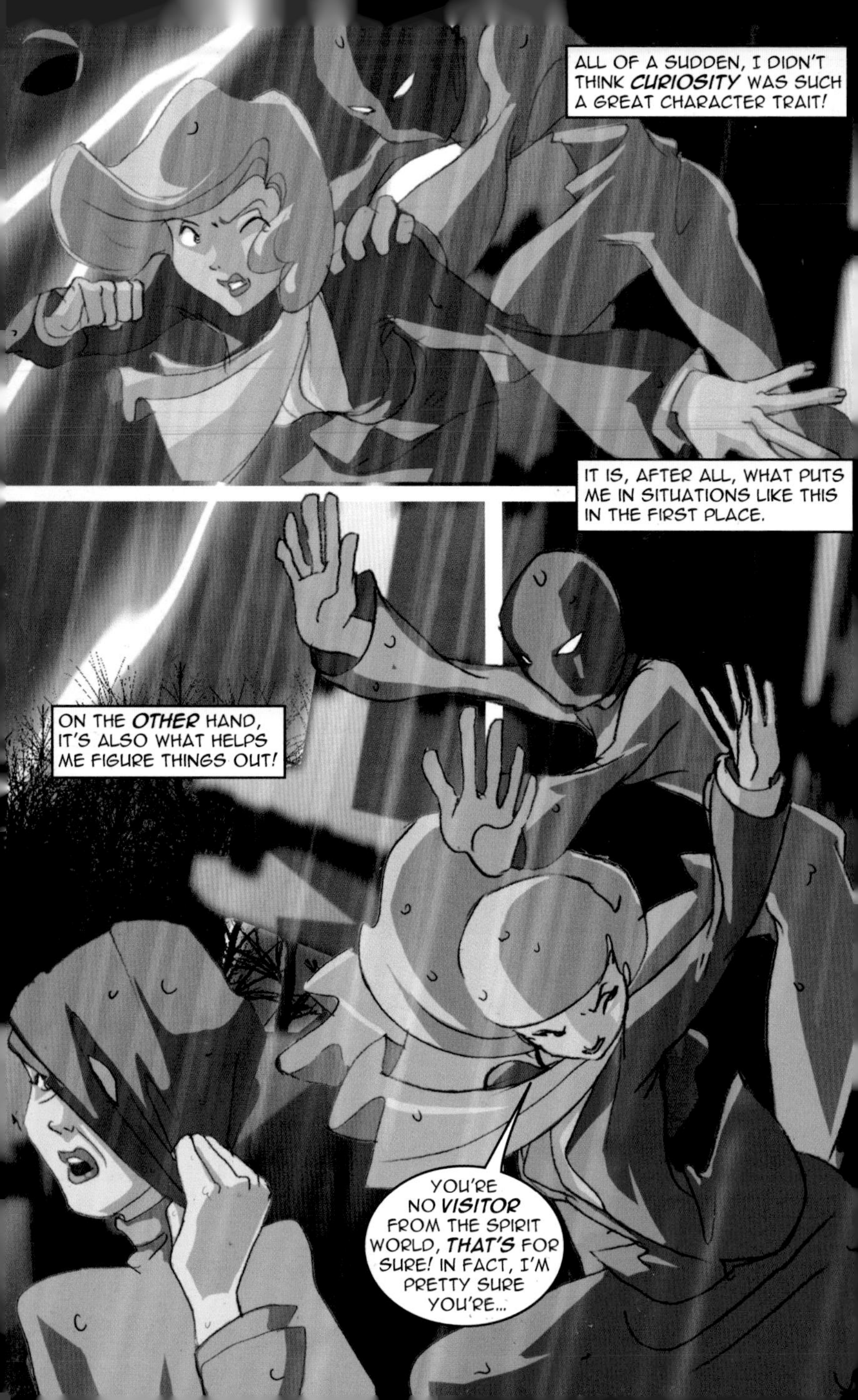
ALL OF A SUDDEN, I DIDN'T THINK CURIOSITY WAS SUCH A GREAT CHARACTER TRAIT!
IT IS, AFTER ALL, WHAT PUTS ME IN SITUATIONS LIKE THIS IN THE FIRST PLACE.
ON THE OTHER HAND, IT'S ALSO WHAT HELPS ME FIGURE THINGS OUT!
YOU'RE NO VISITOR FROM THE SPIRIT WORLD, THAT'S FOR SURE! IN FACT, I'M PRETTY SURE YOU'RE...

EMMA BLAVATSKY!
BUT WHY DO YOU WANT EVERYONE TO THINK YOUR DOLLHOUSE IS HAUNTED?
BECAUSE, YOU SILLY CHILD, I'M BROKE AND NEED MONEY! LOTS OF IT!
WHEN PEOPLE BELIEVE THE DOLLHOUSE IS HAUNTED, I'LL SELL IT FOR A FORTUNE, ALONG WITH THE BOOK AND MOVIE RIGHTS!
I SMUGGLED MY NEPHEW RAUL INTO THIS COUNTRY TO HELP. HE WAS HIDDEN IN THE BASE, REARRANGING THE DOLLS!
"THEN HE WOULD SNEAK OUT AND PERFORM THE CRIME!"
"I TOLD HIM NOT TO WEAR THAT STUPID BRACELET, BUT IT CONTAINED AN IVORY CHARM HIS MOTHER GAVE HIM, SO HE REFUSED TO LISTEN!"

SO YOU'RE CONFESS-ING?

WHY NOT? YOU WON'T BE AROUND TO TELL ANYONE!

UH-OH.

AHHHHHHHHH!

HELP ME! HELP!
IT'S KIND OF SAD HOW PEOPLE WHO ARE TRYING TO KILL YOU ONE MINUTE, SOMETIMES BEG YOU FOR THEIR LIVES THE NEXT.

I'M SORRY! I CONFESS! I DON'T EVEN BELIEVE IN AN AFTERLIFE! IT WAS ALL A LIE! I JUST DON'T WANT TO DIE!

THANKS FOR THE CONFESSION, BUT I WOULD'VE SAVED YOU ANYWAY.
SOME OF US AREN'T KILLERS, YOU KNOW.

I JUST WANTED MY GOLDEN YEARS TO BE COMFORTABLE! I CAN'T BELIEVE I WAS ACTUALLY WILLING TO KILL FOR THAT!
I PUT SOME GAS IN YOUR CAR TO BRING IT HERE. WE'LL USE IT TO GO TO THE POLICE.
NO MORE TROUBLE FROM ME, I SWEAR!
REMEMBER HOW I SAID I WAS TRUSTWORTHY?

NO MORE TROUBLE FROM ME ONCE YOU'RE DEAD THAT IS, YOU LITTLE FOOL! HA!
WELL, SOME PEOPLE JUST AREN'T!

RAUL, THERE YOU ARE! HELP ME WITH THE GIRL!
WE CAN CARRY HER BACK UP AND THROW HER OFF THE ROOF! THE PLAN WILL STILL WORK!

I'M AFRAID HE'S NOT IN ANY POSITION TO DO THAT, MRS. BLAVATSKY.
BUT I **DO** THANK YOU FOR CONFESSING TO ATTEMPTED **MURDER**! IT WILL MAKE A NICE **ADDITION** TO THE CRIMINAL CHARGES THAT WILL BE FILED AGAINST YOU!

NO!
GOOD TO SEE YOU, CHIEF McGINNIS, AS ALWAYS!

BUT HOW DID YOU **KNOW** TO COME OUT HERE? RAUL KNOCKED OUT YOUR OFFICER RIGHT **AFTER** HE RADIOED TO TELL YOU EVERYTHING WAS **QUIET**!
AH, BUT I RECEIVED **ANOTHER** CALL!

TA-DA!
BEST FRIENDS TO THE RESCUE! WE KNOCKED OUT RAUL AND CALLED CHIEF McGINNIS!
AND WE DIDN'T EVEN HAVE TO BREAK FAITH WITH NOSTALGIA WEEK TO DO IT! BETWEEN MY MECHANICAL SMARTS AND GEORGE'S TECHNICAL SAVVY, WE REWIRED THIS OLD 1930s PHONE!
I GUESS THE NEW OWNER TURNED ON THE PHONE SERVICE, BECAUSE WHEN WE PLUGGED IT IN, IT WORKED!
MAYBE GEORGE AND I SHOULD OPEN OUR OWN DETECTIVE BUSINESS!
OR AT LEAST A REPAIR SHOP! BUT THANKS, GUYS!

I GUESS I'LL NEVER UNDERSTAND SOME OF THE IDEAS PEOPLE COME UP WITH IN THEIR DESPERATION! THE FUNNY THING ABOUT EMMA BLAVATSKY'S CRAZY SCHEME WAS THAT IT ALMOST WORKED!
STILL, DESPITE THE TROUBLE, NOSTALGIA WEEK WAS A SUCCESS, RAISING OVER $200,000 FOR CHARITY!
GEE, THE WEEK IS BARELY OVER, AND GEORGE IS ALREADY BACK ON HER CELL PHONE!
CLEARLY, SHE'S MORE COMFORTABLE IN THE 21ST CENTURY.
YOU BET! THANK HEAVENS THAT ANCIENT ANTIQUE WEEK IS OVER!
I'M TAPPING MY HEELS TO BE TAPPING MY KEYBOARD AGAIN!
TAP-TAP-TAP-TAP

I STILL CAN'T BELIEVE HOW BESS THOUGHT THOSE DOLLS WERE REALLY HAUNTED! HOW SILLY CAN YOU GET?
YIIEE! IT'S A DOLL! OF ME! GET IT AWAY! GET IT AWAY!
IT'S JUST A TOY I MADE FOR YOU, GEORGE! WHAT'S THE MATTER? THINK IT'S HAUNTED?
THE PAST IS A WONDERFUL PLACE, FULL OF EXCITEMENT AND MYSTERY, BUT IN THE END, I ALWAYS LIKE TO REMIND MYSELF...
THERE'S NO PLACE LIKE THE PRESENT!
THE END

Special Advance Preview of NANCY DREW Graphic Novel # 4 – "The Girl Who Wasn't There"
NANCY DREW HERE, DEALING WITH A DIFFERENT KIND OF MYSTERY–THE MYSTERY OF MODERN TECHNOLOGY!
I THINK COMPUTERS ARE TERRIFIC – EXCEPT WHEN THEY DON'T WORK.
GEORGE COULD CLEAR THIS UP IN A MINUTE, BUT SHE AND BESS WERE AT A FAMILY REUNION IN OHIO AND I DIDN'T WANT TO DRAG HER AWAY FROM THE PARTY.
AGHHH!
THE GIRL WHO WASN'T THERE
CHAPTER ONE:
HERE, THERE AND EVERYWHERE!

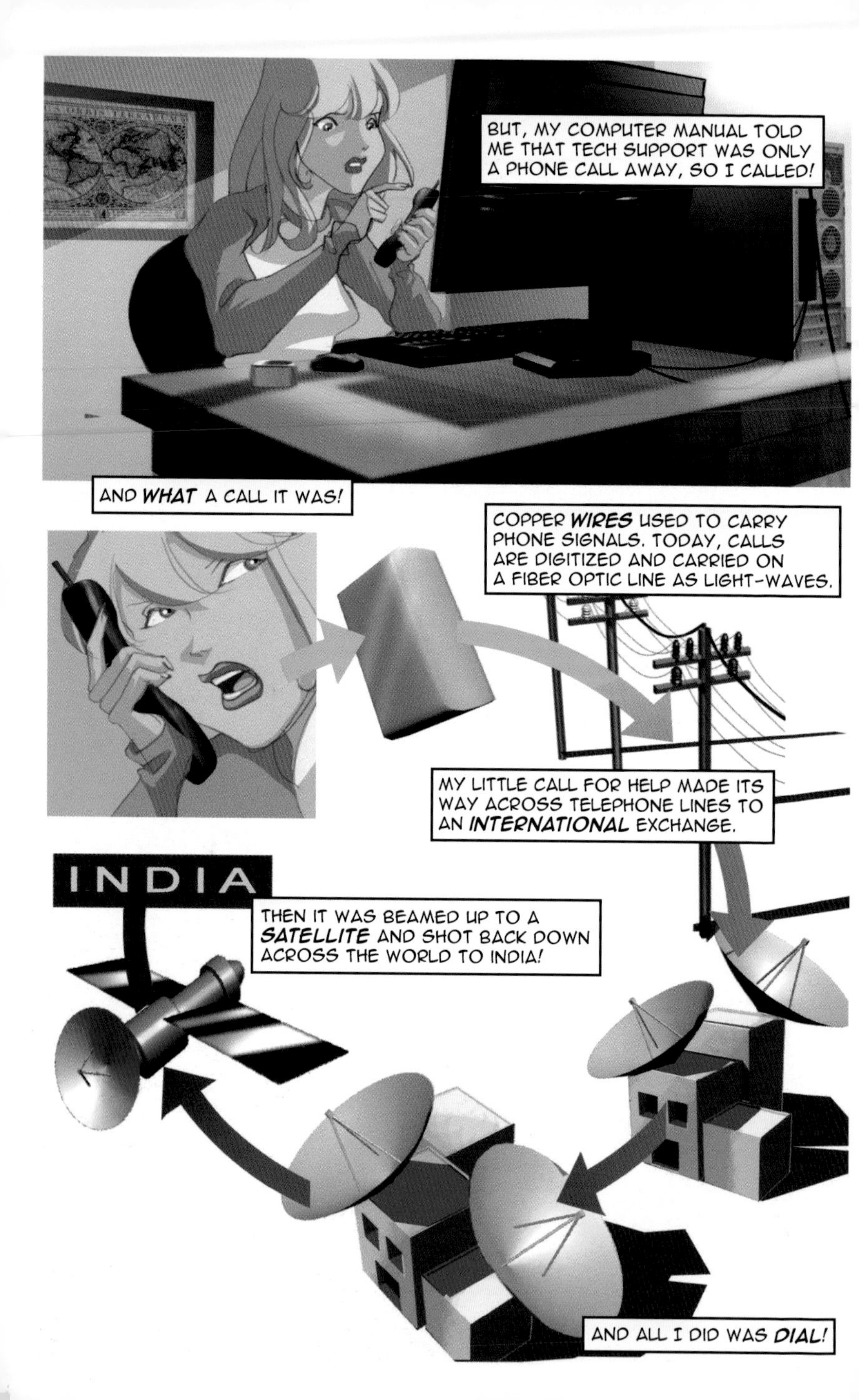
BUT, MY COMPUTER MANUAL TOLD ME THAT TECH SUPPORT WAS ONLY A PHONE CALL AWAY, SO I CALLED!
AND WHAT A CALL IT WAS!
COPPER WIRES USED TO CARRY PHONE SIGNALS. TODAY, CALLS ARE DIGITIZED AND CARRIED ON A FIBER OPTIC LINE AS LIGHT-WAVES.
MY LITTLE CALL FOR HELP MADE ITS WAY ACROSS TELEPHONE LINES TO AN INTERNATIONAL EXCHANGE.
INDIA
THEN IT WAS BEAMED UP TO A SATELLITE AND SHOT BACK DOWN ACROSS THE WORLD TO INDIA!
AND ALL I DID WAS DIAL!

NANCY DREW, YES, I HAVE YOUR RECORDS HERE. LOOKS LIKE YOU'RE DUE FOR AN OS UPDATE.
PLEASE HOLD ON WHILE I TAKE CARE OF THAT FOR YOU!
IT'S FIXED! HOW CAN I **THANK** YOU?
WELL, YOU COULD TELL ME IF YOU'RE NANCY DREW THE GIRL **DETECTIVE**, WHO I LIKE TO READ ABOUT ON THE WEB!
WOW, I HAD **NO** IDEA PEOPLE HAD HEARD OF ME, BUT I GUESS SOME OF MY CASES ARE PRETTY FAMOUS. WHERE ARE YOU LOCATED?
WELL, SINCE YOU ASKED, I CAN TELL YOU I'M IN NEW DELHI, INDIA!
YOU NEVER KNOW **WHEN** YOU'LL MAKE A NEW FRIEND, OR **WHERE**.

OVER THE NEXT FEW DAYS, KALPANA AND I GREW CLOSE!
GEE, WE LEAVE FOR A FEW DAYS, ANDIT'S LIKE WE'RE REPLACED BY A PHONE PAL!
SO YOU'RE A DETECTIVE, TOO? I CAN'T BELIEVE HOW MUCH WE HAVE IN COMMON!
AS I SAID, MY DAD'S AN UNDERCOVER DETECTIVE. SOMETIMES I HELP HIM ON HIS CASES.
WOW!
OH, LEAVE HER ALONE, GEORGE! TO TELL YOU THE TRUTH, KALPANA SOUNDS LIKE SOMEONE I'D LIKE TO MEET, TOO!
YOU'RE RIGHT - THE FRIENDSHIP WILL PROBABLY BE OVER AS SOON AS NANCY GETS THE NEXT PHONE BILL!
BUT IT'S NOT LIKE WE COULD DROP BY AND JUST SAY HELLO!

THINGS DID SLOW DOWN WHEN THAT PHONE BILL ARRIVED, BUT WE STILL EMAILED EACH OTHER A LOT.
UNTIL ONE NIGHT, AT 3:00 IN THE MORNING, MY CELL RANG.
BRPPP BRPPPP

HELLO?
NANCY, IT'S KALPANA! THERE ARE MEN IN MY HOUSE, I THINK THEY WANT TO KIDNAP ME!
I DIDN'T KNOW WHO ELSE TO CALL! SOME OF THE POLICE HAVE BEEN BRIBED I...

AIEEEEEE!
HELLO? HELLO?
KALPANA?!

AFTER MY CALLS TO THE NEW DELHI POLICE GOT ME NOWHERE, I KNEW I SOMEHOW HAD TO GO HELP KALPANA *MYSELF*.

FORTUNATELY, MY FATHER HAD BEEN PLANNING TO VISIT INDIA, TO MEET A CLIENT WHO PRODUCES FILMS.

FIGURING I'D NEED ALL THE HELP I COULD GET, I GOT HIM TO SPRING FOR TICKETS FOR BESS AND GEORGE, THOUGH I FOUND MYSELF WISHING THEY WOULD STAY IN *THEIR* SEATS, NOT *MINE*.

BUT WHAT WOULD I DO WHEN WE GOT THERE?

OH, I LOVE FLYING! IS *THAT* INDIA?
NO, THAT'S A CLOUD.

I DIDN'T EVEN KNOW KALPANA'S LAST NAME, OR WHAT SHE *LOOKED* LIKE!

Don't miss NANCY DREW Graphic Novel # 4 – "The Girl Who Wasn't There"

THE HARDY BOYS

ON SALE NOW!

ALL-NEW STORIES! ALL-NEW FULL COLOR COMICS!

A NEW GRAPHIC NOVEL EVERY 3 MONTHS!

Graphic Novel #1
"The Ocean of Osyria"
ISBN 1-59707-001-7

Graphic Novel #2
"Identity Theft"
ISBN 1-59707-003-3

Graphic Novel #3
"Mad House"
No sooner do Frank and Joe Hardy rescue a top British secret agent, then they're off on a new top-secret ATAC (American Teens Against Crime) mission. Joe and Frank must go undercover on a new reality TV show called "Madhouse," to see how far the producers are willing to go to risk the lives of their teen contestants for the sake of huge ratings. But then the producer of Madhouse turns up murdered!
ISBN 1-59707-010-6

All: Pocket sized, 96pp., full color, $7.95
Also available in hardcover!
$12.95 each.
Vol. 1: ISBN 1-59707-005-X
Vol. 2: ISBN 1-59707-007-6
Vol. 3: ISBN 1-59707-011-4

THE HARDY BOYS
#3 MAD HOUSE
UNDERCOVER BROTHERS
Scott LOBDELL
Daniel RENDON
based on the novels of Franklin W. Dixon
PAPERCUTZ

The Hardy Boys: Undercover Brothers™ Simon & Schuster

AT BOOKSTORES NOW!

PAPERCUTZ

WWW.PAPERCUTZ.COM

At your store or order at: 555 8th Ave., Ste. 1202, New York, NY 10018, 1-800-886-1223 (M-F 9-6 EST)
MC, VISA, Amex accepted, add $3 P&H for 1st item, $1 each additional.

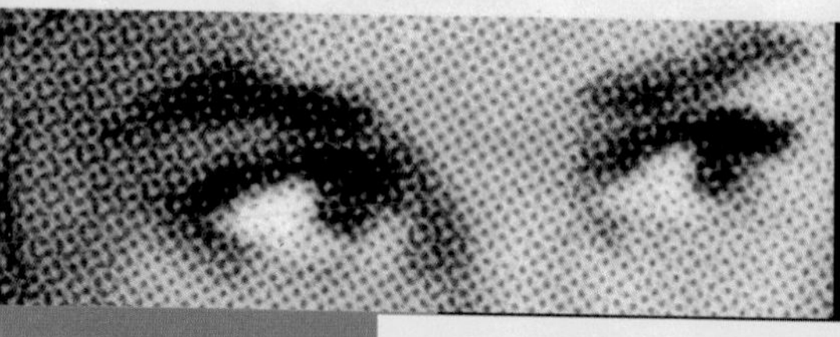

GET A CLUE

Smarter

Cooler

Quicker

Hipper

Surer

Braver

Faster

Newer

Nancy Drew © S&S, Inc.

READ NANCY DREW

girl detective ™

New mysteries every other month—
Collect them all!

Super Mystery #1:
Where's Nancy?

New in November 2005:

#14
Bad Times, Big Crimes

Available wherever books are sold!

Aladdin Paperbacks • Simon & Schuster Children's Publishing
www.SimonSaysKids.com